Jump, Tamika, jump!

Tamika began to rock—front, back, front, back—riding the rhythm of the whirling ropes and spreading spaces. Pumping herself to run in.

Pickles called to her, "Hurry up! Run in, girlfriend! You wearin' out my arms!"

The ropes crossed. The ropes crisscrossed. The ropes opened and closed in front of Tamika, like a sideways eggbeater.

"Whooo!" Tamika was in the ropes, in the air, in the rhythm.

First Stepping Stone Books you will enjoy:

By David A. Adler
(The Houdini Club Magic Mystery series)
Onion Sundaes
Wacky Jacks

By Kathleen Leverich
Brigid Bewitched

By Mary Pope Osborne
(The Magic Tree House series)
Dinosaurs Before Dark (#1)
The Knight at Dawn (#2)
Mummies in the Morning (#3)
Pirates Past Noon (#4)

By Barbara Park
Junie B. Jones and the Stupid Smelly Bus
Junie B. Jones and a Little Monkey Business
Junie B. Jones and Her Big Fat Mouth
Junie B. Jones and Some Sneaky Peeky Spying

By Louis Sachar
Marvin Redpost: Kidnapped at Birth?
Marvin Redpost: Why Pick on Me?
Marvin Redpost: Is He a Girl?
Marvin Redpost: Alone in His Teacher's House

By Marjorie Weinman Sharmat
The Great Genghis Khan Look-Alike Contest
Genghis Khan: A Dog Star Is Born

By Camille Yarbrough
Tamika and the Wisdom Rings

Tamika
and the
Wisdom
Rings

by Camille Yarbrough

illustrated by Anna Rich

A FIRST STEPPING STONE BOOK

Random House 🏠 New York

*Tamika sends her thanks
to her big spiritual sister, Susan Taylor*

Text copyright © 1994 by Camille Yarbrough.
Illustrations copyright © 1994 by Anna Rich.
Library of Congress Cataloging-in-Publication Data
Yarbrough, Camille. Tamika and the wisdom rings / by Camille Yarbrough;
illustrated by Anna Rich. p. cm. "A First Stepping Stone book."
SUMMARY: Tamika finds strength in her family, her friends, and herself as she
copes with the murder of her father by drug dealers.
ISBN 0-679-82749-8 (trade) — ISBN 0-679-92749-2 (lib. bdg.)
[1. Afro-Americans—Fiction.] I. Rich, Anna, ill. II. Title
PZ7.Y1955Tam 1994 [E]—dc20 93-39477

Manufactured in the United States of America 10 9 8 7 6 5 4 3 2 1

Random House, Inc. New York, Toronto, London, Sydney, Auckland

Contents

Tamika

and the

Wisdom Rings

Sweet Fruit

Tamika was upset about what happened to the Community Room.

She loved the Community Room. It was on the first floor of the building where she lived. Every Friday after school the Sweet Fruit of the African Family Tree Club met there.

Tamika was one of the Sweet Fruit.

She loved being a Sweet Fruit.

The African Family Tree Club had a volunteer teacher named Nana Grant. She taught all the Sweet Fruit how to dance African dances and write poetry and draw pictures and make papier-mâché masks. They put the poems and pictures and masks up on the walls. That made the Community Room beautiful.

On this Friday, when Tamika and her friends went into the Community Room, they were shocked.

Somebody had trashed it. It was a mess.

Mr. Harris was the security guard for the building. He said, "Some of them drugged-up kids did it. Just like they did the elevators last month."

Tamika couldn't deal with it. She ran out of the room and into the lobby. Then she pushed open the big glass door and ran outside.

The bus-stop shelter was right in front of the building. Tamika leaned her back against it and kicked the sidewalk.

"Why did they mess up our room?" she wondered. "Why do people act mean and stupid? I wish I could do something to make them behave."

But what could Tamika do?

She was only eight years old, only three and a half feet tall. And in her white, below-the-knees T-shirt, tights, sneaks, and braided, beaded hair, she weighed only sixty pounds.

Tamika's friend Shaniqua came out of the building. She held the door open.

"Why did they tear up our room?" Tamika asked her.

"Gail said Denise said James and Rochelle an' nem did it," Shaniqua answered. "An' you *know* why."

"Yeah." Tamika nodded. "'Cause they're drugheads. My daddy told them don't come in there with drugs. He's the Super. But they don't even listen to him."

"Um-hum," Shaniqua agreed. "But Tamika!

Nana Grant said to come back in the Community Room right away. 'Cause guess what?"

"What?"

"'Cause this is the last time we gonna be in it," Shaniqua whispered. "Your father gonna close it up."

"Oh no!" Tamika said. She ran past Shaniqua into the building.

Bad Changes

The two girls hurried down the hall to the Community Room.

Tamika stopped at the door. She put her hand through the small broken window.

"See," she said. "They broke the glass out."

Tamika and Shaniqua went inside. The Community Room was crowded with children. Nana Grant was at the piano. The children were sitting on the floor in front of her. They were all singing her "Say What You Feel" song.

Little Kwame Phillips told Tamika, "Come on! You missin' it! Say what you feel!"

Tamika was too sad to say anything. All she could do was look at the walls. Everything was spray-painted. The walls, the ceiling, the floor, the piano.

Tamika walked over to Nana Grant.

"They messed up everything," she said. "And now we can't have fun and learn things anymore."

Nana Grant said, "That's not going to happen."

Then she said, "Children, you are going to draw more mag-*nif*-icent pictures, sing more in-spi-*ra*-tion-al songs, write more *shock*-ing poetry, and dance more e-*lec*-tri-fy-ing dances than ever before."

The children yelled and clapped and stamped their feet.

"Don't worry!" Nana Grant told them. "The pot is not broken. It is just cracked a little bit! We will get our Community Room back!"

Tamika's father came into the room. He was waiting for them to finish.

"Stand up, please," Nana Grant told the children. "Let's make our African Family Tree Circle and say our motto. Begin with the seed."

Tamika stood in the circle with the other Sweet Fruit. They laced their fingers together. Then they closed their hands in front of their faces.

"We are born of an old seed!" they said.

"Make the root," said Nana Grant.

Everyone pointed their closed hands to the floor. Then they opened their fingers and put their arms down to their sides like roots in the earth.

"We are growing from a deep root!" they said.

"Make the strong branches," Nana Grant sang to them.

The children raised their arms above their

heads like tree branches, and stretched them to the right and left.

"We are part of a strong branch!" they said.

"Make the fruit!" said Nana Grant.

The children let their hands hang down like fruit from a tree.

"We are the sweet fruit of the African family tree!" they said.

"Make the world," Nana Grant sang out again.

The children circled their arms in front of them.

"Wherever we may go, wherever we may be..."

The children crossed their arms and held hands.

"I am part of you, you are part of me. And the fruit don't fall too far from the tree!"

"Now huuuugg the child next to you!" Nana shouted. "Tell them you love them."

Tamika and the children hugged each other. They did jump hugs and rock hugs.

They hugged Nana Grant and Tamika's father.

Some parents came into the room and the children hugged them too.

When people began to leave, Tamika stayed

behind with her father. He was talking to Nana Grant.

Finally they left the room. Tamika's father picked up a flat piece of wood. He began to nail it over the broken window in the door.

Tamika didn't want to see him do it. She pushed the button for the elevator. The door opened and Tamika got in. She pushed the button for the third floor.

The elevator went up, then stopped on the second floor.

Two teens got on.

Tamika said, "What's up, James? What's up, Rochelle?"

"Nothin'," they said. "What's up wid chu?"

Tamika frowned. "I was wondering about something. Why you all tear up the Community Room? An' take drugs?"

James's face was blank and chilled when he looked at Tamika.

"Who said we take drugs?" he said. "Who said we tore up that ol' room? It wasn't nothin' no how. What you wonderin' 'bout us for?"

"I was wondering about you," Tamika said, "because Gail said Denise said you all got mad because my Daddy said don't come in there with drugs. So you and your friends tore up everything. That's stupid."

Rochelle pushed Tamika against the wall. "Who you callin' stupid, Stupid? You better talk about some'um you know."

Tamika pushed her back. "Don't put your hands on me, Rochelle. You not my mama."

The elevator door opened and Tamika backed out.

Rochelle held the elevator door.

"You act like you tryin' to be grown," James told Tamika. "You better keep your mouf shut or ah'm gonna deck you."

He let the door close.

Tamika stood in the hall looking at the closed door. She was trembling.

"Ah'm gonna deck you too," she whispered. "You changed."

Then Tamika turned and ran down the hall to the apartment where she lived.

The Tamika Express

The next morning Tamika went down to the laundry room in the basement with her mother and her fourteen-year-old sister, Ronnie. They washed two big bags of clothes, then got on the elevator to go upstairs.

The elevator stopped on the first floor and they saw Nana Grant. She was on her way to take some of her homemade pies to a church dinner.

Mama said, "Can you come upstairs for a minute, Nana?"

Nana said, "Yes!"

Tamika was glad when Nana came up to talk, and sad when she didn't stay long.

After Nana left, Mama gave Tamika a job to do.

Tamika had to match the clean socks, then ball them up so Mama could put them away.

Tamika emptied the bag of socks onto the front-room couch and started to match them. But then her imagination took over.

She played puppet with the socks. She put a sock on each hand.

One sock said, "You talk too much, Tamika. Why you wonderin' about us? You think you grown. Ah'm gonna deck you!"

The other sock said, "I don't think I'm grown neither! You tore up our room. That's stupid! I'm too through with you! I'm gonna deck you too."

Ronnie was in the hallway with Mama putting clean laundry in the closet.

"Look, Mama," she said. "Tamika's playing puppet 'stead of doing what you told her."

Mama looked at Tamika and laughed.

"Tamika," she said, "you're never going to finish. Oh, look!"

Mama pointed to the plastic bag on the coffee table. "Nana Grant left her pies. Quick, Tamika. Run downstairs and give them to her. Maybe she's still in the building. Be careful. Hurry up."

Tamika dropped the socks and bounced off the couch. She grabbed the plastic bag and was gone out the apartment door.

Nana Grant was still in the lobby. She was at the security desk talking to Mama on the telephone.

Tamika held the bag behind her back and tiptoed up behind Nana. She tapped her on the hip.

"Guess what you left?" she asked.

Nana laughed into the phone. "She's here already...Yes, the Tamika Express just arrived. Joyce, you saved my life. If I got there without these pies, you would never see me again. They would run me out of town."

Nana put her arm around Tamika's neck and gently pulled her to her side. "Yes, I'll tell her. See you later."

Nana hung up the phone and turned to Tamika.

"Mika, you are faster than a laser beam. Are the pies still in the bag?"

"Yes!" Tamika held the bag out in front of her.

"Tamika, I have a message for you. Your mother said stay down here at Mr. Harris's desk. They're coming down to go shopping. So you wait right here. Can you keep an eye on her, Mr. Harris?"

Mr. Harris was on the phone. He nodded.

Nana bent down to hug Tamika good-bye.

Tamika whispered, "I'm gonna miss our club meetings."

"Thank you, Tamika," said Nana. "I know I'm going to miss you, too. But we have to deal with some problems in this building. Your father will straighten it out. We'll have class again."

"Nana?" Tamika continued to whisper. "I was wondering about something. Do you have a few minutes so I can tell you something important?"

"Always. Come right over here."

Wonder!

There were two chairs near the wall opposite the security desk. The young people in the building called them the Old People's Chairs because only the elderly were allowed to sit in them.

Nana sat down.

"You're too young," she told Tamika. "But you're with me, so sit down."

The chairs were old metal office chairs with green plastic seats, backs, and armrests.

Tamika sat down. Her legs didn't reach the floor.

Gail and Denise ran out of the elevator.

"You ready to jump?" they asked Tamika.

"I can't come now," she told them. "I have to go shopping with my mama."

"Oh no." Gail frowned.

"The Block Rockers Club is gonna beat us if you don't come, Tamika," said Denise. "The Sweet Fruit Club is gonna lose the championship of the block."

"Huh-hunnn. They not gonna beat us." Tamika shook her finger. "For real. When I come back we gon' stomp 'um."

"Okay," Gail called back as she and Denise ran outside.

Tamika looked around the lobby. People were everywhere. The telephone was ringing.

She slid off the chair and leaned against Nana's chair.

"Nana?" Tamika whispered. "People keep telling me I wonder too much. They say—You tryin' to be grown, Tamika."

"Who said that?"

"James and Rochelle. I told them I was wondering why they tore up our Community Room? Why they take drugs? They said I'm trying to be grown. I'm not trying to be grown. I was just wondering why they act stupid."

Nana stared at Tamika, then up to the ceiling. Her mouth opened and closed, but she didn't say anything. Then she shook her head and said, "You are a blessed child."

Tamika leaned in closer.

Nana went on. "What you did in that elevator was dangerous. Dangerous. Do you hear me? Do not ever accuse anyone of taking or dealing drugs. Do not ever accuse anyone of tearing up our Community Room. People who will do those things will hurt you. Grown-ups are supposed to take care of things like that."

Tamika frowned. "But the drugheads tore up the elevator before. And the grown-ups *didn't* take care of it. Nana, you said—A child is the one who gives grown-ups the boldness to speak up in a gathering. But they're not speaking up. They act like they're scared of the teens. I wonder what's wrong with 'um."

Nana Grant looked away from Tamika again.

Tamika watched her swallow. Watched her take a deep breath and slowly rise to her feet. Watched her right arm go up and her right hand tremble in the air.

The whispering was gone now. Nana was gone into a shout.

"Our children are watching!" she shouted.

Everyone in the lobby froze.

All eyes were on Nana Grant.

"She got the spirit," Tamika said.

She had seen this happen before. In Nana's storefront church.

A frowny-faced woman was waiting for the elevator. She broke the freeze. She turned away and said, "Aw, she gon' preach again. Tell me something new."

Others began to move, talk, leave.

The elevator opened. The frowny face went in and Shaniqua came out. She hurried over to stand next to Tamika.

"Nana is shouting," Tamika whispered to her.

Nana continued. "The child was wondering…amen…why…amen…we grown-ups…amen …act like we're scared of our own young ones…amen."

"Amen! Amen!" Tamika and Shaniqua answered.

Every Sunday at church they helped Nana shout. They loved to shout.

Nana Grant spoke louder and began to walk around. "The child spoke the truth about us. We *are* scared. Because we stopped wondering! We grown-ups need to wonder. Wonder how come we're not guiding and correcting our children the way we used to…amen…with love and respect."

"Amen! Amen!" The girls clapped.

"Wonder!" Nana shouted as she stopped in front of the elevator. "Our children are watching us. Our children are wondering what's wrong."

"Amen! Amen! Amen!" The girls jumped up and down.

"The old scriptures say—Know yourself. But we're afraid to know. Afraid to wonder. And our children are watching.

"The old scriptures say—Master yourself. But we are afraid to try. And our children are watching. Amen."

"That's the truth," Tamika shouted. "Amen."

Nana walked the lobby. "When we were a captured and enslaved people, we wondered what it would be like to be free. We wondered

and loved and cared for each other all through the centuries of slavery and the battle of civil rights."

"Tell the truth, um-hum. Tell it, sister," said Mrs. Richardson from the seventh floor. She went to Nana's church.

"We didn't come through all of that to stop loving and caring for each other now. Hold on!"

Nana stretched her arms. "If you don't feel magnificent and noble, wonder how it would feel. And let yourself *feel* magnificent and noble. Then wonder how you can make it real. And *do* it! Wonder it real!"

Tamika looked at the people watching Nana. Some, like Mrs. Richardson, were in the spirit with Nana.

Other people rolled their eyes at Tamika and Shaniqua.

One woman said, "You better stay out of people's business." She didn't say it to Nana

Grant. She just kind of said it in the air as she went out the door.

"I'm having services," Nana said slowly. "Tomorrow at eleven at my church. All are welcome to come."

Tamika heard the familiar sound of heavy footsteps and jingling keys. It was Daddy coming down the hall.

Tamika ran to him and took his hand.

Then the elevator door opened and Tamika's mother and Ronnie came out.

Tamika's mother laughed. "You still here, Nana? I thought you'd been gone."

Nana laughed. She put her purse strap over her shoulder, picked up her bag of pies, and patted Tamika and Shaniqua on the head.

"Just had to help Tamika with a little problem," she said. "But I'm gone now."

She turned and hurried out the door.

Tamika looked at her father.

"Daddy, can Shaniqua come shopping with us?" she asked. "Her mama's not home again."

Tamika's father and mother looked at each other. They knew that sometimes Shaniqua's mother stayed away all day.

"Sure. Come on, Niqua," Daddy said.

The two girls smiled at each other and ran out the front door.

"I'll be back in an hour," Daddy told Mr. Harris. "Goin' to the supermarket."

Outside, Daddy called Tamika. She was walking in front with Shaniqua.

"What problem was Nana helping you with?" Daddy asked her.

Tamika put her hands in her pockets and looked down at the ground.

"Daddy asked you a question," Mama said.

Tamika's voice was low when she answered. "I made a mistake."

Daddy asked, "Well?"

Tamika told him, "Gail said Denise said that James and Rochelle take drugs. She said they tore up the Community Room. When I got on the elevator last night I saw James and Rochelle. I asked them why they take drugs, and why they tore up our Community Room."

Ronnie frowned at Tamika. "You stupid."

"Hush, Ronnie," Mama said. "What did James and Rochelle say?"

"They said they didn't do it. They said I talk too much. They pushed me."

Daddy said, "They pushed you? Who? Who?"

Mama patted Daddy on the back. "Be cool, baby."

"But I pushed them back," Tamika said. "Then I got off the elevator."

Daddy stopped walking. He took Tamika by the shoulders and turned her around. He bent down to face her.

"I told you to stay out of the elevators by yourself! People do all kinds of things in those elevators. And how many times do I have to tell you not to talk to anybody about drugs?"

"I forgot, Daddy," Tamika said. "I was just wondering why they act mean."

Daddy said, "Come on. We gonna talk about this when we get home."

They walked on.

Ronnie frowned at Tamika. "You told a *somebody said somebody said* story."

Mama took Tamika's hand.

"You are going to get yourself hurt, Tamika. I told you how dangerous *somebody said somebody said* stories are. You never know if they are true or not. Don't you remember what happened to your cat?"

"Some kids threw her out of a window," Tamika said. "Because somebody said somebody said cats always land on their feet when they fall."

"Was that story true?" Mama asked.

"No," Tamika answered. "Rita got hurt. An' she got mad at strangers. Now she bites 'um, like a pit bull dog. So we changed her name to Pit Bull."

"Didn't you promise me something, Tamika?"

"I promised not to repeat *somebody said somebody said* stories. But I forgot, Mama. I'm sorry."

Tamika was glad when they came to the supermarket.

Go-fers

Shaniqua ran in first and pulled the shopping cart out of the rack.

Tamika asked, "Can we push it, Mama?"

Ronnie sucked her teeth.

"Yes. Go over to the vegetable section first," Mama said.

Tamika and Shaniqua pushed the cart in that direction.

"My mama don't like vegetables," Shaniqua informed everyone. "She likes fruit, though. She likes kiwi and things like that. I wish I had some money. I would buy my mama some kiwi. You know what that is?"

Tamika's mind was not on what Shaniqua was saying. She shook her head.

"Mama says kiwi comes all the way from Australia," Shaniqua explained. "It's a little like a lemon. But it's brown on the outside. When you cut it open, it's real green on the inside. It's got about a million little seeds in it and it tastes kinda like lemonade that don't have enough sugar in it."

Tamika heard Shaniqua. But she was busy wondering if Mama and Daddy were still mad at her. She thought, "I don't think I'm going to ask them to buy me anything this time."

Mama picked out some collard greens, potatoes, and onions.

"Meat section," she said.

Tamika and Shaniqua pushed the cart over to where the meats were.

"My daddy is a meat-and-potatoes man,"

Tamika said. She finally smiled. "He says he doesn't like fancy stuff, just meat and potatoes. Like that." She pointed to a steak.

"My mama likes shrimp and lobster," said Shaniqua. "She don't hardly eat no meat."

Tamika made a face. "Lobsters scare me. They're red and got big claws like this."

She opened her hands like claws and snapped them at Shaniqua.

Shaniqua ran to the front of the cart to get away.

"Okay, go-fers," Mama said. "I'm gonna put you to work now."

"Yes!" the girls answered.

Mama and Daddy called out what they wanted. The two girls hurried from aisle to aisle reading the signs and finding things. Soap powder, toilet paper, paper towels, bread, honey, peanut butter, frozen pizza, cooking oil, ketchup, hot sauce.

Finally the cart was full and they headed for the checkout line.

Tamika and Shaniqua didn't want to wait in line. They went to the row of vending machines near the door. The machines were full of plastic balls with toy rings and bracelets inside.

"I want that one and that one," Tamika announced.

Shaniqua picked out hers too.

"Come on, yaw," Ronnie said as she went out the door with Mama. "We gonna leave you."

Tamika and Shaniqua squealed and ran after them.

But Tamika didn't see Daddy outside. So she and Shaniqua ran back into the store to look for him.

He was at the toy machines. They ran to him. Daddy put money in the machine. Tamika cupped her hands to catch the plastic balls as they came out.

"Don't try it," Daddy said. He held his large hand in front of hers and caught the toys.

"Give me mine," Tamika pleaded as she followed him out of the store.

Daddy laughed and put the plastic balls into his pants pockets. "Wait till we get home, Mika. We're going to have a talk and we're going to have a party."

Tamika and Shaniqua clapped. "Par-tee! Par-tee!" They ran ahead to the corner.

When Mama and Daddy and Ronnie finally caught up with them, Mama gave both of the girls some groceries to carry.

"Here," she said. "Make yourselves useful."

The girls took the groceries and hurried toward home.

At last they were at the apartment building. Then in the elevator going up. Then in the kitchen emptying the grocery bags and putting things away.

"We're finished, Daddy," said Tamika.

"Okay, baby," Daddy said. "Everybody into the living room. Par-tee!"

Wisdom Words

Mama carried a tray with a bottle of apple juice and glasses on it. She put it on the coffee table. Daddy carried Pit Bull. Shaniqua came in carrying a can of nuts. Ronnie carried a cake.

They all sat down on the couch.

Daddy said, "You young ladies need some guidance so you will know what to do and what not to do. Now, what you do is guided by what you think. What you think is guided by what you know. Mama and I are going to give you some wisdom words and something to help you remember them."

Tamika, Shaniqua, and Ronnie nodded.

Mama opened the little plastic balls and emptied the rings onto the table.

"Oooh, look." Tamika pointed. "That's a cat face on that ring. That's Pit Bull."

Everyone laughed.

Tamika showed the ring to Pit Bull. Pit Bull smelled it.

Mama separated the rings into three groups.

"Now promise," Mama said, "to remember the wisdom words and let them guide you."

The girls promised.

"Let me see your left hand," Daddy said.

The girls held out their left hands. Tamika's hand was out first.

"The first ring has a bird on it. Let's call it the Flying Bird ring," Daddy said.

Mama put the bird rings on the girls' fingers. "The Flying Bird means a rising, free mind," Mama said.

Tamika tried to imagine her mind flying free like a bird.

"Say the wisdom words after me," Mama whispered. "I will use my gift of thought before I use my gift of action. Think before I do."

The girls repeated the words after her.

"The second ring," Daddy said, "is the Pit Bull ring."

Mama put the Pit Bull rings on their fingers.

Again they repeated the wisdom words.

"No matter how many times I am disappointed or brokenhearted, I will love myself. I will love my people. I will love humanity. I will love my creator and life. And I will hold on to my loves like a pit bull."

41

"Like a pit bull," Tamika said as she squeezed Pit Bull.

"The third ring," Daddy told them, "is the Heart of Truth ring."

Mama put the heart rings on their fingers, and the girls repeated the final wisdom words.

"I am the mother of humanity. I must carry myself with dignity."

"Amen! Amen!" Tamika and Shaniqua shouted. "We got us some rings."

Mama shook her finger at them.

"Are you going to remember?" she asked.

The hall intercom buzzed from downstairs.

Daddy said, "Wouldn't you know it."

He got up to see what it was.

"I gotta go. Somebody's holding the elevator again," he called back to them. "Go ahead. Start the party. Turn on some music. I don't know how long I'm gonna be."

"Aw, naw," Tamika and Ronnie complained.

Daddy went out the door.

"This always happens at the wrong time," Mama fussed. "Okay. Open up the nuts, Shaniqua. Cut the cake, Ronnie."

Mama poured apple juice into the glasses.

Tamika looked at her rings. She tried to remember the wisdom words that went with each one. When she looked up, she saw Pit Bull on the coffee table. The cat was drinking apple juice from one of the glasses.

"Look, Mama!" Tamika laughed.

Mama said, "Get down, Pit Bull." She pushed the cat off the table.

Then the hall intercom buzzed again.

Mama went to answer it.

Suddenly, she screamed and ran out of the apartment.

The Scary Movie

The three girls ran out into the hall. They could hear Mama running down the stairs.

Ronnie slammed the door shut and locked it. They all ran down the stairs.

The lobby was crowded with people trying to look into the elevator.

Tamika was frightened. She didn't see Mama or Daddy.

Then she heard Mama scream. Mama was in the elevator.

Tamika and Ronnie pushed their way

through the crowd of people. They stopped at the elevator door.

Tamika couldn't believe what she saw. Daddy was in the elevator, on the floor. Mama was kneeling next to him.

Daddy was bleeding. Daddy was shot.

Tamika's eyes were wide open. She watched the ambulance come and take Daddy to the hospital. Mama went with him.

Ronnie held Tamika's hand. The two girls stayed with Mr. Harris's wife for the rest of the day. Late that evening, Nana Grant came and took them to their apartment. Mama was home. She was in bed.

"The doctor gave your mother something to make her sleep," Nana told them. "When she wakes up, she will tell you about your daddy."

Early the next morning, Mama came to

their bedroom. Her voice was tired. She told them Daddy was dead.

"Some drug people were selling drugs in the elevator. When Daddy told them to get out, they shot him and ran away."

Tamika and Ronnie cried. Mama put her arms around them.

Tamika didn't eat much breakfast. Most of the day she slept and held Pit Bull. When she woke up, she went to the hall closet. She found the clean socks and played puppet.

The first puppet said, "Tamika, you talk too much. What you said to James and Rochelle in the elevator made the drug people mad."

The other puppet said, "That's why they shot your daddy. It was all your fault. Don't ever ask questions again."

On Tuesday Mama took Tamika and Ronnie to the funeral home to see Daddy for the last time. Tamika and Ronnie and Mama sat in the front row of chairs. Tamika didn't look at Daddy. She just kept whispering, "I'm sorry. I'm sorry, Daddy."

Nana Grant, Mr. and Mrs. Harris, and some other neighbors were there too. They came over to shake hands with Mama.

Tamika felt sad and frightened and nervous all mixed up together.

Tamika thought, "I feel like I'm in a movie."

She felt like all the people in the room were in the movie too. And she was watching the movie from her seat next to Mama and Ronnie.

It was a strange feeling.

When the other people talked, she couldn't hear them very well. But everything she was thinking was loud. It sounded like her thoughts were talking to her.

She saw one of the teens from her building come in. His name was David. He used to help

Nana Grant in the Community Room. But when he started taking drugs, he stopped helping.

Tamika watched him try to shake hands with Mama.

And she heard herself thinking, "Oooh! Mama slapped him into tomorrow! Mama is breaking! Mama is fighting! Maybe he might shoot Mama."

And she heard herself saying, "Don't you hurt my mama! Mama! Mama!"

Tamika watched herself get up and try to come between Mama and David.

She watched Nana and Ronnie and some other people pull Mama one way and David another way.

She watched Mama push David out into

the hall. She heard Mama say, "Look, David! Look at what you're doing. Killing everybody! Look in these other rooms. In every room a dead young person is laid out in a coffin. All because of your drugs! Look at 'um!"

Tamika felt someone grab her arm. It was Nana Grant. She held on to Ronnie too.

"Stay with me," she told them. "It's going to be all right, babies."

Tamika closed her eyes and held on to Nana. After a while, Mama stopped screaming.

When Tamika opened her eyes and looked around, David was gone. Someone was putting Mama into a car.

"Come on," Nana said. They got into the car behind Mama's.

Tamika was very tired. In the car she snuggled under Nana's arm. Before they reached the apartment building, she was asleep.

Tamika changed after that. She still wondered about things. And she still had questions to ask. But she didn't ask them.

Mama changed too. She used to be calm. Now everything got on her nerves.

When Mama saw the drug people, she screamed at them. "You killed my husband. You're killing our people!"

One day one of the drug people grabbed Ronnie and told her, "Ya mama got a big mouth. We gon' get Tamika and you and her. Tell ya mama we said *move*. Yesterday. Move."

That night somebody shot through their window.

The next day Mama found a new apartment.

Little Sticks

The night before they moved, Nana came to help them pack. They were packing the pots and pans when the doorbell rang.

It was Shaniqua.

Shaniqua smiled. "I came to help you pack."

Tamika smiled back. "Come on."

Tamika took Shaniqua into her bedroom. She had one big suitcase and two little ones. They started packing Tamika's clothes in the big suitcase. When Shaniqua saw Tamika's Sweet Fruit of the African Family Tree Club T-shirt, she started to cry.

"I don't want you to go," she said. "You're my best, best friend."

"We're always gonna be friends," Tamika told her. "Don't worry. I'm gonna give you my phone number. We can call each other every day. Promise?"

"I promise." Shaniqua wiped her eyes. "We're gonna be friends forever."

"Why can't people just stay together till they get old and die?" Tamika asked. "I'm gonna miss Daddy forever, and you and Nana and our friends. Why do things have to change all the time?"

"I don't know," Shaniqua answered.

Tamika sat down on the bed. "Mama said some changes are good and some are bad. She said we got some bad ones. But we're gonna get some good ones too."

Shaniqua smiled. "Let's look for the good ones. I'm gonna look for 'um every day!"

Tamika nodded and closed her eyes. "I'm gonna pray for 'um. Amen."

"Amen," said Shaniqua.

When they finished packing, Shaniqua helped Tamika take the suitcases to the front hall.

Mama and Nana Grant and Ronnie were sitting on the couch.

"Girls, come over here," Mama called to them. "Nana wants to tell us something."

They sat down on the floor in front of the couch.

Nana said, "This is a story that was told to me. Now it's my place to tell it to you."

Nana gave each of them a bundle of little sticks. Each bundle had a string tied around it.

"Try an' break the bundle," Nana told them.

Tamika tried hard to break hers. She couldn't. Mama couldn't break hers, either. Nobody could break their bundle of little sticks.

"Now open the string and take one of the little sticks out." Nana showed them how to do it. "Try to break the stick."

Tamika broke one of the sticks. Then another one. Everyone broke a stick.

"Now you see?" Nana explained. "When we're all together, like that bundle of little sticks in your hands? When we're all tied up with the string of love? Then *nothing* can break us apart. But what happens when you take the love away? What happens when you take the sticks out a piece at a time? You can break them.

"Now, your loving daddy and husband is gone," said Nana. "But before he left, he wrapped his love around you like that string is wrapped around those little sticks. And as long as that love stays there, nothing can break you apart."

Mama got up and hugged and kissed Nana. Tamika and Ronnie and Shaniqua hugged her too. Even Pit Bull rubbed against her legs.

A Family Good-bye

Tamika got up early the next morning.

She fed Pit Bull and put her in her carrying case.

The moving men came, and soon everyone was carrying something downstairs.

Tamika took Pit Bull down last. She put the case on the backseat of Mama's car. That was where she was going to sit.

The truck and the car were full.

Mama said, "Come on. Let's say good-bye to the Harrises."

Mama, Tamika, and Ronnie went back inside the building. Mr. Harris and his wife were in the lobby. They smiled and kissed cheeks and shook hands with Mama, then Ronnie.

When they tried to kiss Tamika, she turned away.

"I don't want to say good-bye," Tamika said.

Mama took Tamika by the hand. "Come on, Mika," she said.

Then Nana Grant came out of the stairway door.

She said, "Wait! Wait!"

Behind her came all the children in the Sweet Fruit of the African Family Tree Club. They marched into the lobby. Shaniqua was with them.

Tamika was surprised.

The children made the African Family Tree Club Circle around her and Mama and Ronnie.

They gave Mama and Ronnie flowers.

They gave Tamika a book of their poems and drawings.

"This is especially for you, Tamika!" Kwame said when he gave it to her.

"Say what you feel," Nana Grant told them.

The children began to shout.

"We love you, Tamika!"

"We love you!"

"We're sorry your daddy died."

"We're sorry you have to move."

"We love you, Tamika!"

Tamika couldn't say a word. She wanted to tell them that she loved them too. But all she could do was look up at Mama.

"Let's say our motto," Nana Grant whispered.

Tamika and Ronnie and Mama joined the circle. Tamika stood next to Shaniqua. The children said their motto.

"We are born of an old seed!" They made the seed.

"We are growing from a deep root!" They made the root.

"We are part of a strong branch!" They stretched their arms like branches.

"We are the sweet fruit of the African family tree!" They dangled their hands like fruit.

"Wherever we may go, wherever we may be…" They made the world.

"I am part of you. You are part of me." They crossed their arms and took hands.

"And the fruit don't fall too far from the tree!"

Then all the children hugged Tamika. Tamika was hugging back. They hugged Tamika through the doorway and into the car.

The Cage

Tamika walked up the stairs behind Mama. She was carrying Pit Bull in her carrying case. Ronnie walked behind her.

"This is a brownstone building," Mama told them. "We have apartment 3B on the third floor."

Mama unlocked the door and Tamika followed her inside.

The apartment was one room with a window in the the back wall. Tamika went over to it. She put Pit Bull's case down and looked out into the yard below. All she could see were the windows and backyards of other apartment buildings.

She sat on Pit Bull's case and looked around the room.

"I don't like this place," she thought. "It's too little for us. The sink and stove are in between the front door and the closet. The bathroom is in the back of this ol' apartment. You can look in it when you come in the front door."

Ronnie came in. Her arms were full of clothes.

"It's a kitchenette," Ronnie said.

Mama frowned at her. "This is not a kitchenette, Ronnie. I hate kitchenettes. This whole floor used to be one big apartment. The owner cut it in half. This is the back half I'm paying all this two-job rent for."

Mama sounded angry.

The moving men were coming up the stairs with the pull-out couch. Mama walked out into the hall to show them the way.

She had sold some furniture, given some away, and put some in storage.

Tamika was to sleep on the pull-out couch with Mama. Ronnie on the fold-up rollaway bed.

When the furniture was all in, the moving men were gone, and the door was closed, Tamika looked from Ronnie to Mama.

No one spoke.

Only Pit Bull meowed. She wanted out of her cage.

New Friends

The day after they moved, Tamika went to the laundromat with Ronnie and Mama. It was across the street from their new apartment building.

Two girls Tamika's age were in the laundromat. One was helping her mother. The other was helping her grandmother.

They smiled at Tamika.

But Tamika was not ready to make new friends yet. She didn't smile back.

While their clothes were washing, the girls

went outside and jumped Double Dutch. Tamika watched them from the window.

The next day Tamika and Ronnie went to their new schools. Tamika saw the two girls from the laundromat. They were in her class.

They looked at Tamika. Tamika looked at them.

Everybody asked, "Hi, what's up?" But nobody answered.

The teacher wrote on the blackboard:

A Poem About Me

"Write a poem about yourself," she said to Tamika. "When you read it to us, we'll get to know you."

Tamika remembered the call-and-response songs she learned in the Sweet Fruit of the African Family Tree Club.

She wrote a call-and-response poem.

My name is Tamika
I just moved to this neighborhood
I'm almost nine years old
I just moved to this neighborhood
I have a mama, and a sister
    named Ronnie
She goes to the high school next door
I just moved to this neighborhood
I jump Double Dutch big-time
I just moved to this neighborhood
So, hi from Tamika
I just moved to this neighborhood

Everybody loved Tamika's poem. They clapped and told her they were happy she came to their school.

At lunchtime Tamika didn't want to play in the schoolyard. She felt like being quiet. She felt like being alone. And she felt like hollering.

She went outside and sat on the steps.

The girls from her neighborhood were jumping rope.

One of them came over to her.

"Tamika, you wanna jump?" she asked.

Tamika was looking at the girl. But she was thinking about Shaniqua and her friends in the old neighborhood.

"What's the matter?" the girl said.

Tamika didn't answer.

"My name is Ebony," the girl said.

"Yeah," Tamika answered. "I remember when you said it in class."

"You wanna jump with us?" Ebony asked her.

Tamika got up. She and Ebony walked over toward the other girls.

The girls were arguing about who was turning wrong.

Tamika walked over to one of the turners. Her name was Melody.

Tamika said, "Let me turn."

Melody handed Tamika the ropes.

Tamika turned real evenhanded.

The other turner smiled at Melody and Ebony. She said, "Um-hum."

"It's your turn, Pickles," Melody said.

"Who's Pickles?" Tamika asked.

Ebony was rocking to run in. She said, "That's me."

Melody said, "She's got a thing for pickles."

Tamika smiled.

Pickles jumped goin' on.

When she finally made a mistake, the other girls clapped and yelled.

Pickles said to Tamika, "I want to see *you* jump."

Tamika pointed to the other turner. "It's her turn."

"Naw," the girls said. "We want to see you jump."

Tamika gave Pickles the ropes. She made sure Pickles was holding them right.

The girls began to turn the ropes. Then they started singing.

Jump, Tamika, jump
Jump, Tamika, jump
Jump, Tamika
Jump, Tamika
Jump, Tamika, jump

Tamika looked down. She kept thinking about Daddy. She wanted to cry.

Jump, Tamika, jump

Tamika began to rock—front, back, front, back—riding the rhythm of the whirling ropes and spreading spaces. Pumping herself to run in.

Jump, Tamika, jump

Pickles called to her, "Hurry up! Run in, girl-friend! You wearin' out my arms."

Jump, Tamika, jump

They were turning the ropes like turning machines.

The ropes crossed. The ropes crisscrossed. The ropes opened and closed in front of Tamika, like a sideways eggbeater.

"*Whooo!*" Tamika was in the ropes, in the air, in the rhythm.

She hung in space like Michael Jordan.

Her sneakers beat the concrete like Papa Ladji beats the Djeme drum.

Her knees rose and fell, rose and fell. Free and flying like Jackie Joyner-Kersee running for Olympic gold.

She did the front knee rock, the sideways rock. She crossed her legs in front, in back.

She bent over and touched the ground, turned on one leg, turned on the other. Then she

did a simple jump straight up and down and sang
a song the jumpers in her old neighborhood sang.

My name is Tamika and I'm the best
When you jump with me,
You don't get no rest
When I'm up, I'm up
When I'm down, I'm down
Tamika is a girl that don't play around
Touch head and shoulders, baby
One, two, and three
Touch head and shoulders, baby
One, two, and three
Head and shoulders
Head and shoulders
Head and shoulders, baby
One, two, and three

Tamika ran out. The girls threw the ropes
down.

"OOOO-oooh! OOO-ooh! You jump goin' on!" Pickles said. "Where you learn that song? You have to teach it to us."

Tamika was out of breath and walking around.

She was crying.

The jumpers were confused. They looked at each other.

"Why you crying?" Melody asked.

With the back of her hands Tamika wiped the tears from her face.

"'Cause I feel like it," Tamika said quietly.

She walked back to the school building.

Tamika Remembers

After school, Tamika waited for Ronnie.

Tamika walked behind Ronnie and her new friends. Pickles and Melody came running up and walked with her. At first they just looked at each other, but didn't talk.

Then Melody asked, "How come you cried after you jumped? What's the matter?"

Tamika walked on a while. Then she told her new friends, "I have a lot of things on my mind."

Melody nodded. "I do too sometimes. Ask ya mama. Maybe you can come over ma house sometime. My grandmother is real nice. Maybe you can go to church with us sometime. You go to church?"

"Yes. A friend of mine has a church. A storefront church. She lives in my old neighborhood."

"Do you preach?" Melody asked. "I preach."

"You preach?" Tamika was surprised.

"Yes! That's what ah'm going to be when I grow up," said Melody. "A preacher. Ah'm going to preach the word of God. Ah'm going to bless everybody."

"That's what my friend Nana says. She's a preacher. She called me a blessed child."

Melody nodded. "You *are* blessed, girl. You the boss when you jump rope. When the teacher asked questions today you knew all the answers. You are truly blessed."

Tamika looked at Pickles. "You preach too?"

"No. Ma mama and daddy don't go to church. But they let me go sometimes with Melody. We're in the Junior Choir together."

As they walked, Melody and Pickles looked at Tamika's hair.

They came to their block. Pickles said, "Your braids are goin' on. Who braided 'um?"

"My sister." Tamika smiled and pointed to Ronnie. "There she is up there."

Tamika shook her head and the tiny bells and beads braided in her hair tinkled.

"I want to get me some bells," Pickles said.

"Me too." Melody touched the beads and bells in Tamika's hair.

Tamika showed her friends how they were put on. They saw the rings on her fingers.

"Tamika, you got three play rings," Pickles said.

Melody pointed at the rings. "That one's a cat face."

"Yeah, that's Pit Bull," said Tamika.

Pickles and Melody were surprised. They looked at each other, then at Tamika.

"You got a pit bull?" they asked.

"No, my cat is named Pit Bull."

"Phew. Ah'm glad of that." Melody made a scared face. "Ah'm scared of pit bulls. We got some in our building. People sellin' drugs got two pit bulls like guards. In your building too. Sellin' drugs."

Tamika stopped walking. "What?"

Ronnie heard what Melody said. She stopped and turned around.

"Somebody selling drugs in our building?" she asked.

The story began to fly out of Melody's mouth. "They use drugs. I don't know if they sell them. This woman and her husband. They have two sons, Wallace and Trevor. Wallace is the one that takes the drugs."

Ronnie threw her bookbag on the ground. She was rigid with anger. Tears rushed from her eyes.

Tamika ran to her, squeezed her around the waist. "Ronnie, don't get upset! We don't know if it's true yet. It might be a *somebody said somebody said* story. Ronnie, please. Don't cry."

Ronnie began to wipe her eyes. Melody picked up her bookbag and held it until Ronnie was ready to take it.

Tamika let go of Ronnie and walked by her side.

"No. No way," said Tamika. "Might be just a *somebody said somebody said* story. But we're gonna find out. Right, Ronnie?"

"Yeah," Ronnie answered.

"See you tomorrow," Tamika called to Pickles and Melody. Then she and Ronnie crossed the street and went into their building.

Growin' Up

Ronnie and Tamika ran up the stairs to their apartment. Ronnie had the key. She opened the door.

She went right into the bathroom and closed the door.

Tamika stood outside the bathroom. She could hear Ronnie crying. She wanted to go in and comfort her. But she knew Ronnie wanted to be by herself.

Tamika took off her bookbag and put it in the puff chair. Then she went to the refrigerator

and took out some frozen fish and mixed vegetables and put them in the sink to thaw.

Pit Bull rubbed against Tamika's leg, asking
for food. Tamika fed her.

Then she took her books out of her bookbag
and sat down on the couch to do her homework.

Tears fell onto her notebook paper. She
wiped them away and went on doing her homework.

When she heard Mama's footsteps in the
hall, she dried her face, got up, and opened the
door.

Mama stopped in the doorway when she
saw Tamika's face. Then she rushed into the
room and looked around.

"Where's Ronnie? What happened?"

"She's in the bathroom crying, Mama."

Mama tried the doorknob. It turned and she
went in.

Tamika went to the closet and took out three folding TV tables. She set them up in front of the couch and puff chair.

Then she set three places for dinner on the TV tables.

She could hear Mama talking to Ronnie. Ronnie wasn't saying much.

When Mama came out of the bathroom with Ronnie, she didn't say much either. She just put her shoulder bag and jacket in the closet and started cooking dinner.

Tamika and Ronnie did their homework while Mama cooked.

Tamika showed Mama her homework paper. Mama looked at it. She put her fingers on the raised spots where Tamika's tears had fallen.

"This is good work, Mika," Mama told her. "Just write it on a fresh piece of paper."

At dinner Tamika told Mama, "I made some new friends today."

"See. I knew you would." Mama's smile showed all of her teeth.

"I did too," Ronnie said.

"Go on!" Mama gave them a high five. "What did I tell you? I know my girls are always going to come out on top."

"Guess what?" Tamika leaned toward Mama. "My new friends told Ronnie a *somebody said somebody said* story. That's what made Ronnie feel bad. I remembered what you told me. And I told Ronnie don't feel bad, because we don't know if it's true or not. Didn't I, Ronnie?"

Ronnie nodded. "Yeah. She remembered. She reminded me."

Mama put her knife and fork down and smiled at Tamika.

"You listened. You remembered. You growin' up, girl!" Mama blew Tamika kisses. Tamika blew kisses back.

"We're going to celebrate tonight when I come home," Mama promised. "You did good, girls."

Mama had two jobs now. One during the day. One at night.

Tamika asked, "Mama, can I call Nana after we do the dishes?"

"Yes. Both of you can make some calls, but do not hang on the phone. You know how my money is. It isn't."

When Mama was ready to go to her second job, she stopped at the door.

"Come here, girls." She kissed them. "I don't want you to go out to play yet. Next week. I know you made some friends, but I have to check out this block and meet your friends' parents. So be patient. Finish your homework. Read or look at TV. Give me a kiss. I'm gone."

After the dishes were done, Tamika called Nana.

"Guess what, Nana," she said. "I have two new friends. One's named Melody. One's named Pickles. Melody's gonna be a minister just like you. She told me I'm blessed just like you did…I like them too…Yeah…Thank you. Are you coming to see us?…Okay. I miss Shaniqua. I tried to call her, but her phone was disconnected…Oooh. She can call me. Yeah. I miss you."

Tamika put her hand around the telephone mouthpiece and whispered into it. "Ronnie's feeling sad, Nana. You want to say something to make her feel better?…Okay.

"Ronnie! Nana wants to talk to you! Bye, Nana."

Tamika handed Ronnie the phone. She sat down on the floor and began unbraiding her hair.

After Ronnie finished talking to Nana, she sat down on the couch. Tamika sat between her

legs. Pit Bull walked over and sat on Tamika's lap.

"Put some more bells on, Ronnie, please," said Tamika. "My new friends like my hair. They want you to braid their hair too. With bells and beads."

"They have to pay me," Ronnie said. "Keep your head still. How am I gonna braid?"

"Pay you?"

"For real. Mama gets paid when she does hair. She's a businesswoman. I can be a business-woman too. So tell them they have to pay me."

"How much?"

"Five dollars. I'll give them something easy for five dollars."

"With bells."

"Girl, bells usually cost more, but 'cause they're your friends I'll give them a discount. And if you get me more heads to do, I'll give you fifty cents for each one."

"You will?"

"Turn around! You gonna have some funny-looking braids. So, is that a deal? Fifty cents for each head you get me."

"That's a deal. Ronnie, I'm gonna get you lotsa heads. We gonna make money!"

"You got that right. We gonna help Mama. Ah'm gonna open up a shop for Mama and me."

Tamika stroked Pit Bull and thought for a while. Then she said, "I don't know what I want to be yet. Yes I do! I want to be a preacher or a psychiatrist, something like that. People need a lot of talking to so they feel better. I like to talk to people. You feel better, Ronnie?"

"Yeah."

"Daddy used to talk to us all the time," said Tamika. "He talked to everybody. Made 'um feel better."

Ronnie said, "He talked to you more than he

talked to me. 'Cause he liked you better. 'Cause you were the baby."

Tamika turned around and looked up at Ronnie.

Ronnie made a face at her. "Hold still. Ah'm gonna do your braids backwards."

"You don't like me, Ronnie?" Tamika asked.

"Yeah, I like you," Ronnie answered. "You my little bigheaded sister."

"Daddy didn't like me more than you," Tamika told Ronnie. "He was always telling me to do like you do. He told me—Do like Ronnie."

"He did?"

"Yeah."

When she finished, Ronnie put a stocking cap on Tamika's hair.

Tamika was sleepy.

She took off her sneakers, lay down on the couch, and fell asleep. She dreamed about

Melody and Pickles and jumping rope.

The dream started in front of the building where she lived. Pickles and Melody were turning rope for her. They turned fast.

The ropes whipped out of their hands and stretched up into the air, still turning.

Tamika was in the middle. Then Pickles and Melody came into the ropes with Tamika. All of them were jumping in space.

The ropes turned still faster. They whipped around so fast they mixed Tamika and Pickles and Melody all up. Like when Mama mixed up chocolate cake batter in a bowl.

They whipped around and out and away up into the sky. Melody went someplace. Pickle went someplace. And Tamika went someplace.

They all disappeared.

Sweet Potato Pie

Tamika sat up, frightened.

The room was dark. Only the stove light and the light from the TV were on. A faint moon glow came in through the top of the window. Ronnie was sitting on her bed, braiding her hair and watching TV.

"What's the matter?" she asked Tamika.

Tamika took a deep breath. "I had a nightmare. My friends blew away."

"Blew away?" Ronnie laughed. "You want me to come shake you? You're still sleeping."

The bathroom door opened and Mama came into the room.

"Mama!" Tamika shouted. She ran to her and put her arms around Mama's waist.

Mama was warm from her shower. Her fluffy bathrobe smelled like flowers.

Tamika pressed her nose into the fluff, and took a deep breath to smell the flowers.

"I didn't know you came home, Mama. Why didn't you wake me up?" Tamika complained.

"Because you needed your beauty sleep, girl," Mama teased. "Guess what I brought you and Ronnie? I'll give you a hint. Somebody round, brown, and sweet stopped by the beauty shop and gave me something round, brown, and sweet to give to you."

"Pie!" Tamika shouted. "Ronnie! Nana came by and brought sweet potato pie!"

"Shhhhhh." Mama laughed. "It's late. Now come on. Take the pillows off the couch. Let's put the bed down. Put on your night clothes, Mika."

Mama cut three pieces of pie and put them on napkins. She gave the girls their pieces.

She and Ronnie sat on the side of Mama's bed to eat and watch TV. Tamika stood in the middle of the bed bouncing and eating her pie.

Pit Bull jumped up on the bed and bounced with her.

"Sit down, Tamika," Mama said. "How you gonna eat and bounce at the same time?"

Tamika sat down next to Mama. She pushed her finger into the pie like a spoon and scooped the sweet potato off the crust.

"Mama," she said. "I was wondering about something."

"Serious?" said Mama. "I haven't heard you say that you were wondering about something in a long time."

"I thought you were too through with wondering," Ronnie teased her.

Tamika shook her head. "I didn't stop

wondering. I just didn't feel like telling anybody what I was wondering about. I didn't wanna make trouble."

Mama tucked Tamika's braids beneath her stocking cap.

"You feel more like talking now?" she asked.

"Um-hum. I was wondering. When Ronnie was crying in the bathroom and she told you maybe some drug people live downstairs? Why didn't you get upset like you did at our old building?"

Mama finished her last bite of pie.

"I did get upset," she answered. "I just didn't lose control of myself this time. Before, when I went off, I was almost crazy because they killed Daddy. I wasn't a good example for you and Ronnie. I can't do that again. I have to control myself because I want you to be in control of yourselves. That's why Daddy and I gave you the rings."

Mama laughed. "I need to get some rings to help *me* remember."

She looked at the rings on Tamika's hand.

"What does the Flying Bird ring help us to remember?" Mama asked. "Help me."

Ronnie touched the ring on the top finger of her left hand. "The Flying Bird is the rising, free mind," she said. "It means I will use my gift of thought before I use my gift of action. Think before I do."

"See," Mama said, "I didn't do that. But if we have trouble in this building, I'm going to be smart. The troublemakers will move, not us."

"Yes!" Tamika said. "I was thinking if we have to move one more time, we might get homeless."

"Noooo! Please!" Mama fell back on the bed, then sat up again. "What does the Pit Bull ring tell us?"

Tamika answered. "No matter how many

times I am disappointed or brokenhearted, I will love myself. I will love my people. I will love humanity. I will love my creator and life. And I will hold on to my loves like a pit bull."

"Yes!" they all said, and hugged. Still hugging, Mama asked, "Quick. What does the Heart of Truth ring teach us?"

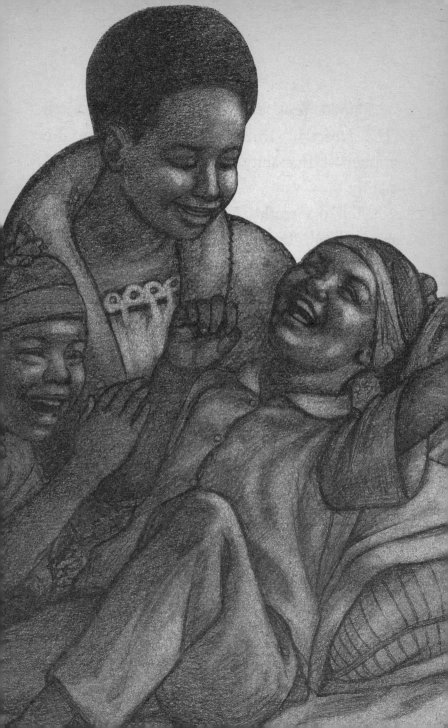

Tamika took a bow before she answered. "The Heart of Truth ring tells me I am the mother of humanity. I will carry myself with dignity."

"Tell the truth!" Mama clapped her hands and laughed. "I'm so proud of you. You remembered."

Tamika saw tears in Mama's eyes. She put her arm around Mama's neck and her head on her shoulder.

"Mama, I was wondering about one last thing."

Mama told her, "Oh, I hope it's not going to be the last, baby."

Tamika began to cry. "Mama, Mama," she whispered. "Did James and Rochelle make somebody shoot Daddy because I called 'um stupid? Did they kill Daddy because of me?"

Mama hugged Tamika.

"No, no, no," Mama whispered to her. "You didn't have anything to do with it."

She looked into Tamika's teary eyes.

"Those drug people shot other people before they shot Daddy," said Mama. "Daddy's death had nothing to do with you, baby."

A sound stopped Mama from talking. Somewhere outside somebody was shooting.

Tamika watched Mama's face become angry. She felt Mama's arm tighten around her.

She saw Ronnie stiffen with fear. She felt herself become frightened again.

"Are grown-ups going to stop being scared, Mama?" Tamika whispered.

Very softly Mama answered, "This one is, baby. This one is."

"Mama, Nana Grant said if you want to change something, you have to wonder it real," Tamika whispered.

Mama nodded. "Nana Grant was right."

Mama wiped her eyes, pressed her hands against her face, and took a deep breath. Then she smiled.

"I'm going to wonder it real—for real," Mama told them. "Big-time! We grown-ups are going to make a wonderful world for you children. But now we have to go to bed so we can get up in the morning and start the change. Before we go to bed, let's share one more piece of pie for Daddy."

In bed, Tamika couldn't go to sleep. She was wondering.

She could see a new Community Room. And children playing and learning things. And the teens dancing and respecting each other. And the grown-ups keeping all the bad things away.

And she saw herself being a preacher or a teacher.

Yes, a teacher.

Then she saw herself telling Pickles and Melody about the Sweet Fruit Club and showing them how to make the African Family Tree Circle and say the motto.

In the darkness Tamika did the movements from the African Family Tree Circle.

"I'm going to wonder it real," she said. "I'm going to wonder it real."

About the Author

Camille Yarbrough knows lots of girls just like Tamika. "They're strong. They're bright. And even though their surroundings might seem hopeless, they are full of hope."

Camille lives and works in Harlem. She is a member of the Black Studies Department at the City College of New York, where she teaches two courses: African Dance and The Harlem Community. She is also a composer, singer, actress, dancer, and—of course—a writer. Her books include *The Shimmershine Queens*, a novel for older readers, and *Cornrows*, a picture book for younger readers.

Camille is the recipient of the Ida B. Wells Award and the Unity Award in Media. She also received a Jazz/Folk/Ethnic Performance fellowship from the National Endowment for the Arts and was named Woman of the Month by *Essence* magazine.